To Ayden on your 6th birthday
From Grandma Jean and Grandad Jim

The Boy Who Changed the World

To

_____

From

_____

Date

_____

Attention Teachers! Visit AndyAndrews.com/Education
for FREE downloadable school curriculum on
The Boy Who Changed the World!

Contact Andy!

To book Andy for corporate events, call
(800) 726-Andy (2639)

For more information, go to
www.AndyAndrews.com

Published in Nashville, Tennessee, by Tommy Nelson. Tommy Nelson is a registered trademark of Thomas Nelson, Inc.

Cover and interior design by Koechel Peterson & Associates, Minneapolis, MN.

Thomas Nelson, Inc., titles may be purchased in bulk for educational, business, fund-raising, or sales promotional use. For information, please e-mail SpecialMarkets@ThomasNelson.com.

Library of Congress Cataloging-in-Publication Data
Andrews, Andy, 1959-
  The boy who changed the world / Andy Andrews ; illustrated by Philip Hurst.
     p. cm.
  Summary: Beginning with Norman Borlaug and going back to those who influenced him directly or indirectly, shows how one ordinary boy came to develop "super plants" that helped save billions of people from starvation.
  ISBN 978-1-4003-1605-2 (hardcover)
  [1. Conduct of life--Fiction. 2. Agriculture--Fiction. 3. Borlaug, Norman E. (Norman Ernest), 1914-2009—Fiction. 4. Wallace, Henry A. (Henry Agard), 1888-1965—Fiction. 5. Carver, George Washington, 1864?-1943—Fiction.] I. Hurst, Philip, ill. II. Title.
  PZ7.A5645Boy 2010
  [E]—dc22
                          2010017100
Printed in the United States of America

11 12 13 14 LB 6 5 4

Mfr. Lake Book / Melrose Park, IL / July 2011 / PPO# 123445

The Boy Who Changed the World

ANDY ANDREWS
Illustrated by **PHILIP HURST**

A DIVISION of Thomas Nelson Publishers

NASHVILLE   DALLAS   MEXICO CITY   RIO DE JANEIRO

*Dedicated to Austin and Adam Andrews, the
two boys who have already changed my world.
I love you both so very much!*

I want to tell you a story about the boy who changed the world. His name was Norman Borlaug. Norman lived on a farm in Iowa. He loved to play hide-and-seek with his little sisters in their father's cornfields.

Norman was tall and skinny with hair so light it looked like the silk that sprouted from the ears of corn. Norman was very good at hiding in the cornfields.

Norman tiptoed quietly so his sisters couldn't hear him. He crept along until he was just close enough to catch them. . . .

"Gotcha!"

The girls giggled and squealed. "Now you hide, Norman!"

Norman ran to hide in the field, careful not to knock down any cornstalks. Just yesterday his father had reminded him, "You know, son, we're blessed to have all this corn. There are many people in the world who do not have enough to eat."

What would it be like to be hungry all the time? Norman wondered as he looked at the endless rows of corn. *There has to be a way this corn can feed the hungry people*, he thought.

Right then and there,
Norman decided to change the world.

Norman learned everything he could about plants. When he was grown, he worked for a man named Mr. Wallace. Mr. Wallace said, "Norman, I want you to use what you learned in school to make special seeds. Those special seeds will grow into super plants and feed more people than ordinary plants!"

To make the special seeds, Norman had to go to faraway places and work in the rain and summer heat, but he never gave up. Finally, Norman developed the special seeds that grew into super plants!

Norman's special seeds of corn and wheat and rice were sent all over the world. Those special seeds grew into super plants that fed the hungry people—just like Norman dreamed about as a boy. And guess what? Norman saved more than two billion people from starving.

Two billion!

It's true...Norman was the boy who changed the world!

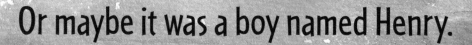

Or maybe it was a boy named Henry.

I want to tell you a story about the boy who changed the world. His name was Henry Wallace. Henry's father was a professor, and one of his students was a young man named George.

Henry loved to go with George on expeditions in the countryside. George knew more about plants than anyone Henry had ever known.

Henry peered over the edge of the water to inspect a plant growing on the bank.

"Don't get too close to that water, Henry," George said. "Your daddy will have a fit if you get eaten by a hippopotamus."

Henry laughed. "Hippos don't live in Iowa! I'm just trying to get a better look at this flower."

"You know, Henry, God gave us plants as a way to learn. We can use that knowledge to help others. It's a very important mission."

"George, I want that to be my mission. Will you help me?"

"Of course. Remember, Henry, God made you to make a difference. And I believe you will."

Henry learned so much about plants that he grew up to be the U.S. secretary of agriculture. Then, Henry Wallace became vice president of the United States of America! From that important office, Vice President Wallace (you can still call him Henry) continued his mission to learn how plants could help people.

As vice president, Henry wanted to help people around the world grow more food, so he hired a young man named Norman Borlaug—the same Norman who later developed the special seeds that grew into super plants that fed the hungry people!

So you see, because Henry is the one who came up with the idea of special seeds and hired Norman to make them, it was really Henry who changed the world!

Or maybe it was George.

I want to tell you a story about the boy who changed the world. His name was George Washington.

Now before we continue, you must know that he is *not* the George Washington of whom you are thinking. The U.S. President George Washington lived a long time before the *boy* George Washington in this story.

George's father died before he was born, and his mother died when he was very young. But the *good news* is that a nice couple named Moses and Susan Carver adopted George and made him a part of their family.

"Well, George, what have you got there?" asked his neighbor Mrs. McLoyd as she plopped down on a tree stump beside the young boy.

"I'm whittling a crutch for my friend who hurt his ankle."

"Just look at you—creating that from a big old tree branch! George, you've got a sharp mind and a kind heart."

"Thank you, ma'am. But it's not much. Won't take me too long."

"I bet your friend will be mighty grateful for that crutch. You know, George, **little things can make a big difference.** Everything we do matters. Every action you take, even small things, can change the world."

Sure enough, George Washington Carver changed the world. He became a teacher and an inventor. For instance, he invented 266 things from the peanut that we still use today. From the sweet potato, George invented 88 things that we still use today.

But he did something much more important than that.

When George Washington Carver was at Iowa State University, he had a teacher named Professor Wallace. On weekends, George would roam the fields and forests with the professor's six-year-old son Henry, teaching the boy about plants and how many ways they could be used to help people.

Now let's see here…

Norman made the special seeds that grew into super plants that fed the world's hungry people. But he couldn't have done it without Henry, who had the idea to make super plants and hired him. But Henry would not have had the idea without George, who spent so much time teaching young Henry about plants.

So there you have it: George Washington Carver was the boy who changed the world!

Wait…we forgot about his dad, Moses.

I want to tell you a story about the boy who changed the world. His name was Moses Carver. He lived on a farm with his mom and dad way up North.

Moses pulled nails out of some old barn wood while his pet rooster Buzz watched.

"Moses!" his mother called as she walked toward him in the field. **"What are you doing?"**

"Well, I figured if I got these nails out of this wood, we could reuse it for something like patching the chicken coop or building a shed."

"Thank you, Moses. That's a wonderful idea. I'm sure Buzz will appreciate it come winter," she said with a smile.

"He hasn't helped with a single nail!" Moses chuckled.

"You know, dear, every choice you make, good or bad, can make a difference. I'm proud of you for making a good choice today."

When Moses grew up, he married a lady named Susan and, together with a few workers, they managed a farm. They were very happy, but one night some men tried to hurt them. Outlaws called Quantrill's Raiders rode into the farm. They burned down Moses' barn and kidnapped some of the workers.

One of the people they kidnapped was a little boy named George.

Moses had to do something! He searched and searched and finally found young George. Moses traded his favorite horse in return for the little boy.

That night, as Moses walked home (remember, he didn't have a horse), he told George that he would adopt him. Moses also promised to give the boy a new name. As the baby boy drifted off to sleep, Moses whispered, "Good night, little George Washington Carver."

So if Moses hadn't saved George from the outlaws, George wouldn't have grown up to take Henry on walks in the forest. Then Henry wouldn't have become interested in plants and later hired Norman.

Without Henry's idea, Norman wouldn't have developed the special seeds that grew into super plants.

And without the super plants, **two billion people would have nothing to eat.**

It's odd, isn't it? Every time something happens, something else happens. That's called the butterfly effect.

When a butterfly flaps its wings, it moves tiny pieces of air . . . that move other tiny pieces of air . . . that move other tiny pieces of air. In fact, on the other side of the world, they might be feeling a big whoosh of wind—all because a butterfly flapped its wings *here* just a few minutes ago!

That means every little thing YOU do matters:

what you did yesterday, what you do today, and what you do tomorrow. God made your life so important that every move you make, every action you take, matters . . . and not only for you or the people around you. Everything you do matters for everyone and for all time!

When you think about it like that... **WOW!**

That means YOU can be the kid who changes the world!